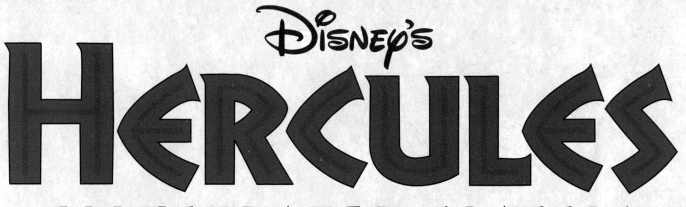

DISNEY'S
HERCULES
ILLUSTRATED CLASSIC

Adapted from the film by
Elizabeth Balzer

DISNEY
PRESS

NEW YORK

We are the lovely muses and we're here to tell you a story about the golden age of ancient Greece: a time of powerful gods and extraordinary heroes. By far, the greatest of these heroes was mighty Hercules, the strongest man who had ever walked the earth. He was, however, acclaimed for much more than his strength.

Our tale begins eons before Hercules' birth, when gigantic brutes called Titans ran amok across the earth. Their mischief caused great chaos: catastrophic earthquakes, tidal waves, and volcanic blasts.

The great Zeus zapped these troublemakers with a hail of thunderbolts, imprisoned them, and brought order to the universe. He organized the gods to rule the rain, sun, and sea and even the passions of mankind. Henceforth, the gods of Mount Olympus looked down on a peaceful planet Earth.

There was great celebration at the palace of Zeus when a son, Hercules, was born to him and his wife, the goddess Hera. All the gods gathered around the infant, who wore a gold medallion and was bathed in a heavenly glow.

After the gods had presented the child with a mountain of lavish gifts, Hera nudged her husband. "But where's *our* gift, dear?"

Zeus formed a puff of clouds with his hands. "We'll just take a little cirrus and a touch of cumulus...."

He spun the clouds into the form of a baby horse, and a white-winged colt stepped out.

"His name is Pegasus, Son," said Zeus. "And he's all yours."

Hercules cooed and gave the horse an affectionate head butt.

The proud father leaned over his son. "So you like your gift?"

Suddenly Zeus was lifted off his feet. The baby had raised him up by a single finger!

"Aha," laughed the proud father. "This child is strong—just like his dad."

As Zeus held his small son, a sinister-looking guest strode through the crowd, scowling. Robed in black, with hair of fire, it was Hades, god of the Underworld.

Zeus greeted him. "So, Hades. How are things down below?"

"Still lotsa room. And lotsa gloom," leered Hades. "And, like always, pretty dead." He snickered at his little joke.

Zeus held out a cup of ambrosia. "How about a little toast?"

"Sorry, old boy. Thanks to you, I've enough toasting to do down below."

Hades swaggered up to the baby. "So there's the little sunspot." From the dark robe he pulled *his* gift, a pacifier shaped like a skull. He tried to stick it into the baby's mouth. "A sucker for the little sucker."

The baby grabbed Hades' hand, holding it in a viselike grip.

"Ouch!" Hades jerked his hand away. "Powerful little tyke."

"He'll be the strongest of all the gods," said Zeus.

Hades rubbed his throbbing hand. "Oh, *will* he, now?" And under his breath he said, "We'll just see about *that*."

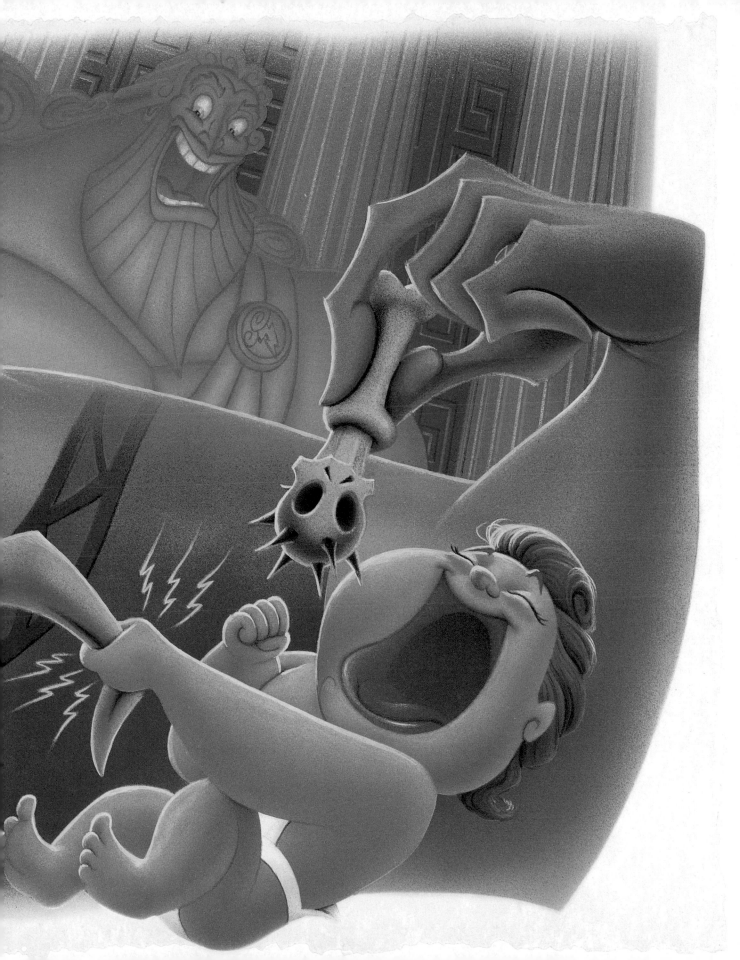

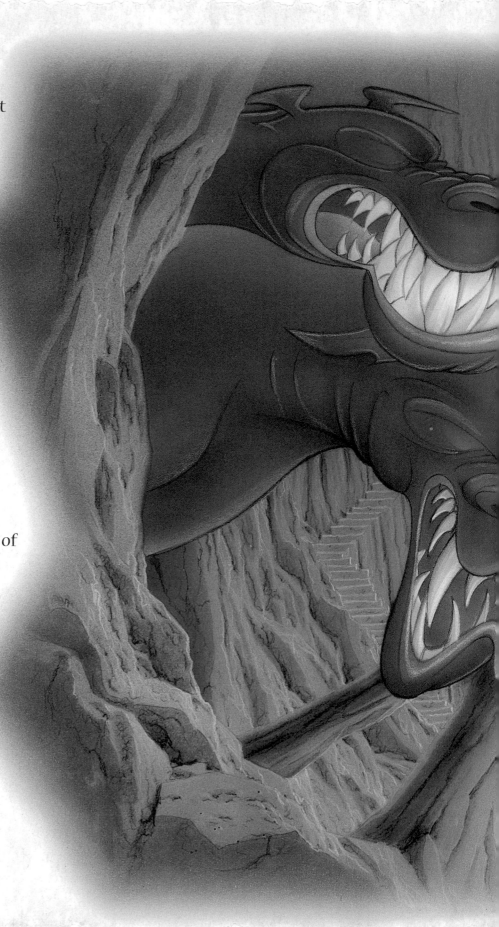

Hades fumed as he drifted down to earth. All the gods on Mount Olympus were whooping it up, devil-may-care, while, thanks to Zeus, he was stuck in the murky mists of the Underworld, sur-rounded by a bunch of dead-heads. "It really burns me up," he grumbled.

By the time Hades had reached the cold, dark shores of the river Styx, his sullen counte-nance had twisted into a crooked smile, one that could only mean—*revenge*!

◆　◆　◆

Charon, Hades' boatman, rowed him along the river of souls to his palace. When the gates of the Underworld opened, Cerberus, a fierce three-headed dog, lunged at the boat, growling.

On the dock stood two small-winged demons. One winced and writhed
as if in constant pain. The other trembled, tail to toenails, as if plagued by
constant fear.

"Pain and Panic," they saluted their master, "reporting for duty."

"Let me know," said Hades, "the instant the Fates arrive."

"They're here already," grinned Panic.

Hades' flames ignited in anger. "THE FATES ARE *HERE?* WHY DIDN'T YOU
TELL ME?"

Pain and Panic fell to their knees. "We are *worms*, Master. Worthless worms." And *poof*, they turned themselves into worms.

Hades ignored them. "Slay you later," he snarled, and turned to greet the Fates, three hideous, beak-nosed crones—Clotho, Lachesis, and Atropos. Having empty eye sockets, the three shared a single eye as they worked, pulling taut and snipping the threads of human lives.

He escorted them into the war room where there was a huge game board of the entire cosmos, with pieces and figures representing Mount Olympus, the planets, and the Underworld, as well as gods, humans, and creatures.

"Sorry I'm late, ladies," Hades said in honeyed tones.

"We knew you would be," rasped Lachesis.

"We know everything," creaked Clotho. "Always."

"Of course," said Hades. "Then you know about Zeus's . . ."

". . . Bouncing baby brat," Clotho finished.

"Right." Blazing inside, but acting cool, Hades asked, "Just tell me. Is this kid gonna mess up my Mount Olympus takeover?"

Lachesis wagged her long finger. "Now, Hades, you know we're not supposed to reveal the future."

Undaunted, Hades turned to Clotho. "Hey, sweetheart. Did you cut your hair? You look fabulous—a Fate worse than death."

Clotho bowed her head and blushed, giggling. As she bent, her eye fell out, *plop*, and bounced like a ball around the room.

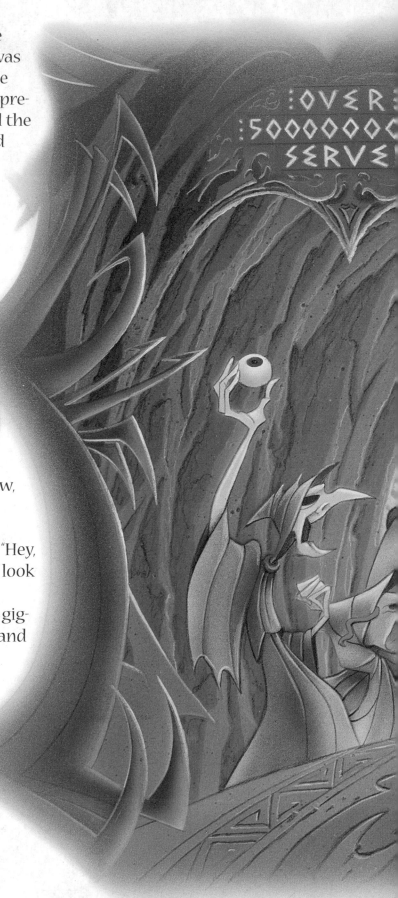

Hades politely returned the eye to Clotho. "Ladies, my fate is in your lovely hands."

Lachesis gave in. "Oh, all right," she sighed. "You win."

Eighteen years hence, chanted the Fates, when the planets were in perfect alignment, Hades would have his chance—his only chance—for action. He would unleash the Titans to bring on the fall of Zeus.

"Yes," intoned the Fates. "The once proud Zeus will finally fall, and you, Hades, will then rule all!"

Hades knocked the figure of Zeus from Mount Olympus and replaced it with a figure that looked like himself. "Yes-s-s! Hades rules-s-s!"

"But," the Fates warned, "a word of caution to this tale. Should Hercules fight . . . you will *fail*!"

With that the eyeball and the crones vanished.

"WHAT?" Hades exploded. With a sputter his flames went out.

When he had cooled down, Hades led Pain and Panic into a nearby room, where a vial of potion floated in a pillar of fire.

"Here's a little riddle," he said. "How do you *kill* a god?"

"You can't kill a god?" guessed Panic. "Gods are immortal?"

"Bingo!" said Hades. "Immortal." He reached for the vial. "So first you've gotta turn the little sunspot mortal!"

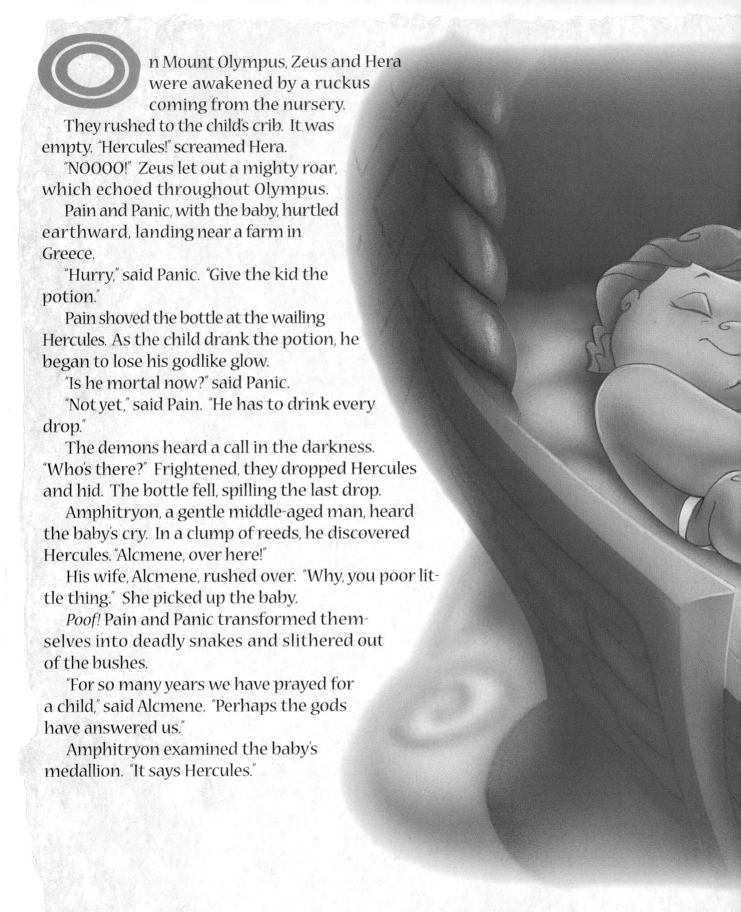

O n Mount Olympus, Zeus and Hera were awakened by a ruckus coming from the nursery.

They rushed to the child's crib. It was empty. "Hercules!" screamed Hera.

"NOOOO!" Zeus let out a mighty roar, which echoed throughout Olympus.

Pain and Panic, with the baby, hurtled earthward, landing near a farm in Greece.

"Hurry," said Panic. "Give the kid the potion."

Pain shoved the bottle at the wailing Hercules. As the child drank the potion, he began to lose his godlike glow.

"Is he mortal now?" said Panic.

"Not yet," said Pain. "He has to drink every drop."

The demons heard a call in the darkness. "Who's there?" Frightened, they dropped Hercules and hid. The bottle fell, spilling the last drop.

Amphitryon, a gentle middle-aged man, heard the baby's cry. In a clump of reeds, he discovered Hercules. "Alcmene, over here!"

His wife, Alcmene, rushed over. "Why, you poor lit-tle thing." She picked up the baby.

Poof! Pain and Panic transformed them-selves into deadly snakes and slithered out of the bushes.

"For so many years we have prayed for a child," said Alcmene. "Perhaps the gods have answered us."

Amphitryon examined the baby's medallion. "It says Hercules."

The couple turned in time to see the snakes about to strike. They froze with fear.

Baby Hercules reached out his tiny hand. *Crunch!* He grabbed the snakes.

"*Yeow! Whoa!*" hollered Pain and Panic, their eyes bulging.

Hercules tied the snakes in a knot, spun them around, and tossed them screaming far into the distance.

Amphitryon and Alcmene stared in shock at the innocent infant, now quietly cooing in the woman's arms.

In the woods, Pain and Panic resumed their demon forms. "We blew it," said Panic. "Hades is gonna kill us when he finds out!"

"You mean, *if* he finds out," said Pain.

✦ ✦ ✦

Because Hercules had not finished the last drop of the potion, he had kept his godlike strength. But Zeus and Hera wept nonetheless because their precious son could never return home ... he was now a mortal.

Adopted by Amphitryon and Alcmene, Hercules grew to young manhood in the tranquil countryside of Greece, though his extraordinary strength often caused problems.

One market day Hercules went with Amphitryon into town. His father left him to stay with their load of barley.

Nearby, some young boys were playing a game of discus. When Hercules asked if he could join them, they refused.

He heard their cruel remarks as they resumed play. "Good old Jerk-ules." "Mr. Destructo."

If they'd just give me a chance, thought Hercules, as he sat alone. A moment later his chance came.

The discus was careening high above him. Hercules, eager to show his skill, leaped thirty feet in the air. "I've got it!"

But he lost control of his momen-tum and *kaboom*, smashed into one of the large stone pillars that sup-ported the market's colonnade. The pillars toppled, one by one, like dominoes, leaving the marketplace a shambles.

The villagers protested to Amphitryon, "Keep that freak away from here." "He's dangerous."

"He's just a kid," said Amphitryon. "He can't control his strength."

"Get him out of here!" chanted the townspeople. "He's a freak, freak, freak!"

"Son, you mustn't let those people get to you," said Amphitryon when they were back on the farm.

Hercules hung his head. "But, Pop, I'm *not* like other people. Sometimes I feel like I really don't belong here. Like I'm supposed to be someplace else."

"Hercules," said Amphitryon, "there's something your mother and I need to tell you."

They sat down with their son and told him how they had found him as a baby. Alcmene showed him the gold medallion. "This was around your neck. It's a symbol of the gods."

Hercules grasped the medallion. "Maybe the gods will have the answers."
He broke into a wide smile. "I'll go ... yes, of course ... I'll go to the temple of
Zeus."

Seeing their sad faces, he put his arms around both of them. "Mom, Pop,
you're the greatest parents anyone could have. You're my family, always will
be. But I just have to know!"

When Hercules reached the temple he approached a colossal statue of
Zeus. He knelt in prayer: "Mighty Zeus, I need to know. Who am I? Where do
I belong?"

With a flash of lightning the statue came alive.

Hercules, frightened, tried to run, but Zeus picked the boy up. "Is this the greeting you give your father?"

"My f-f-father? But I . . . if you're my father," Hercules stammered, "that would make me a . . ."

"A god," said Zeus.

His father told Hercules the whole story. Despite how much Zeus and Hera loved their son, Hercules could not return to Mount Olympus. He was no longer immortal.

"And you can't do anything about it?" asked Hercules.

"I can't, Son. But *you* can." Zeus promised him: "*If you can prove yourself a true hero on earth, your godhood will be restored.*"

"I can do it!" In his excitement Hercules fell out of his father's palm. "But how?"

"First you must find Philoctetes, the trainer of heroes."

"I will!" Hercules sprinted toward the door.

His father grabbed him. "Hold your horses! Which reminds me . . ."

He whistled. Pegasus, now grown, flew in from the sky like a shooting star. "You probably don't remember Pegasus."

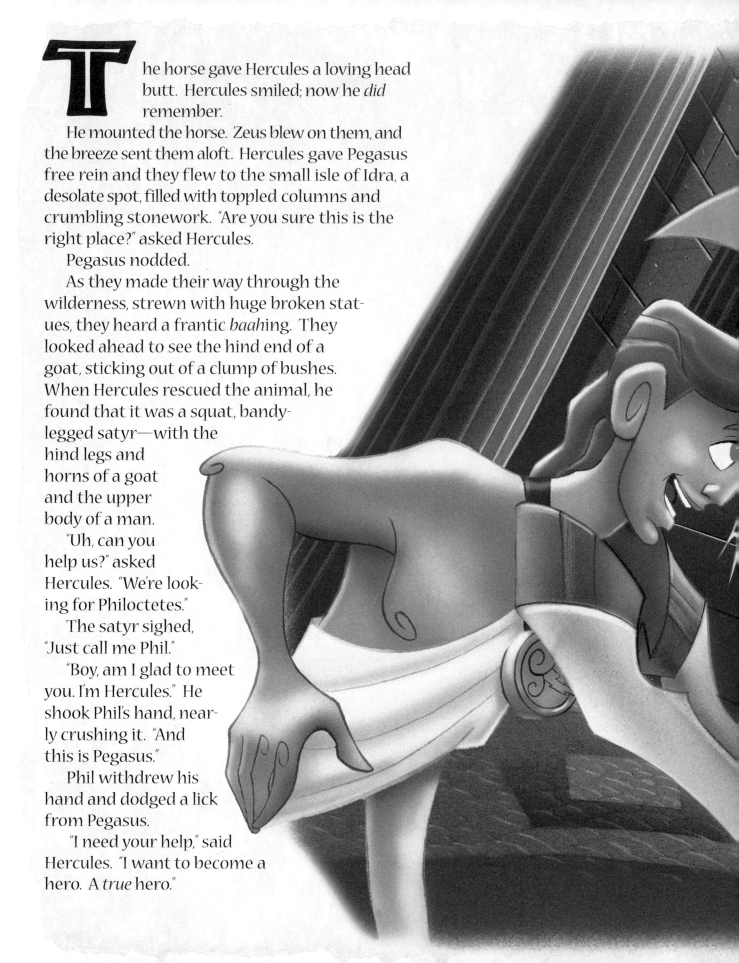

The horse gave Hercules a loving head butt. Hercules smiled; now he *did* remember.

He mounted the horse. Zeus blew on them, and the breeze sent them aloft. Hercules gave Pegasus free rein and they flew to the small isle of Idra, a desolate spot, filled with toppled columns and crumbling stonework. "Are you sure this is the right place?" asked Hercules.

Pegasus nodded.

As they made their way through the wilderness, strewn with huge broken statues, they heard a frantic *baah*ing. They looked ahead to see the hind end of a goat, sticking out of a clump of bushes. When Hercules rescued the animal, he found that it was a squat, bandy-legged satyr—with the hind legs and horns of a goat and the upper body of a man.

"Uh, can you help us?" asked Hercules. "We're looking for Philoctetes."

The satyr sighed, "Just call me Phil."

"Boy, am I glad to meet you. I'm Hercules." He shook Phil's hand, nearly crushing it. "And this is Pegasus."

Phil withdrew his hand and dodged a lick from Pegasus.

"I need your help," said Hercules. "I want to become a hero. A *true* hero."

"Sorry, kid, I can't help you." Phil moved toward a nearby hut. "I'm not in the hero business anymore." He went inside and slammed the door.

"Wait!" Hercules yanked on the knob and *whoosh*, tore the door off its hinges. "Oops, sorry."

Phil put the door back in its frame. "Two words. I'm retired."

But Hercules would not give up. "Look, I gotta do this. Haven't you ever wanted something so badly you'd do anything to get it?"

A look of sadness dimmed Phil's eyes. "Come on in, kid. I want to show you something."

The inside of the hut was crammed with mementos: swords, shields, sculptures, and paintings of former pupils. Phil pointed to them. "I used to dream of training heroes. I was gonna train a hero so famous the gods would hang his picture among the stars.

"But lemme tell you what happened." Phil pointed to the souvenirs as he enumerated all his failures: Odysseus, Perseus, Theseus, Jason. "And to top off my career, there was Achilles." He blinked and looked away. "A guy can only take so much disappointment. Now I know—dreams are for rookies."

"But I'm different. I'm stronger," Hercules insisted. "Just watch." He led Phil outside, where he lifted a huge piece of statuary and flung it into the sea, as if it were a pebble.

Phil appeared impressed but countered, "I'm too old, kid."

"But if I don't become a true hero," said Hercules, "I'll never be able to rejoin my real father, Zeus."

Phil raised an eyebrow. "Sure, sure, kid, your father is Zeus."

"It's the truth!"

"Hmm. Well, even if you were a kid of Zeus's, I'd probably refuse ya. My answer would have to be ..."

A bolt of lightning crashed into their midst, searing Phil. He looked skyward and shrugged, "...Okay!"

The very next day, Phil and Hercules began training— grueling exercises and rescues to test the most courageous youth, especially one who was clumsy and inept. By imposing hundreds of rules, and endless days of practice, Phil finally tempered Hercules' great strength with incredible precision and control. In the process, the two became fast friends.

Hercules was eager to try his new skills. "I'm ready now. I want to battle some monsters, rescue some damsels."

"Take it easy, champ."

"I gotta get off this island, do some heroic stuff."

Pegasus whinnied and stood on his hind legs, as if ready for flight.

Phil looked them over. "Well…"

"Aw, come on, Phil."

"Okay, kid. You wanna road test? Then saddle up. We'll go to Thebes."

Hercules grinned widely as he and Phil soared through the clouds on Pegasus. "So what's in Thebes?" he asked.

"Lotsa nice, juicy problems. Great place for a rookie to build a rep."

They were startled by a woman's scream coming from the river valley below.

Phil peered down. "Just your basic D.I.D.," he said, unimpressed. "Damsel in distress."

Hercules turned Pegasus around.

"Hey, kid, we're going to Thebes. Let's not fool with this routine stuff."

Despite Phil's protests, Hercules headed down to the river.

Peeking through the shore's dense foliage, the trio saw a burly bearded centaur—half man and half horse—chasing a lovely young maiden.

He grabbed her, and she kicked and shouted, "Nessus, put me down!"

"Ooh, Megara, sweetheart. I like 'em fiery."

As they watched the struggle, Phil whispered, "Now remember, Hercules, analyze the situation. Don't just barrel in without thinking."

But when he turned to face the boy, Hercules was gone. He was already confronting the centaur.

"Halt!"

"Step aside, two-legs," said Nessus, rearing up on his hind legs.

Hercules tried to act bold, but words failed him. "Pardon me, my good, uh, sir...."

Megara struggled free of the centaur's arms. "Back off, Atlas," she said to Hercules. "I can handle this."

"But, uh, ma'am ..."

Nessus belted Hercules in the jaw. He sailed through the air into the water and came out brandishing a fish!

Pegasus tried to go to his master's rescue, but Phil restrained him: "Whoa, he's gotta do it on his own."

The fight continued, while Megara looked on in amazement. At length Hercules got the upper hand, sending Nessus zooming into the sky with such force that he lost his shoes.

The centaur descended and crashed into the river, and when he came up for air—*bonk, bonk, bonk, bonk*—all four shoes landed on his head.

"Are you all right, Miss, uh . . . ?" stammered Hercules.

"My friends call me Meg." She gazed up at him. "Did they give you a name—along with those powerful pectorals?"

"I-I'm Hercules, but you can call me Herc."

"I think I'd prefer 'Wonder Boy.'" She turned to leave. "Well, thanks for everything, Herc."

"Wait! Um, can we give you a ride?"

Pegasus gave an angry snort and flew up into an apple tree.

"I'll be all right," she said, scowling at the horse. "I'm a big girl." She smiled and spoke softly, "Bye-bye, Wonder Boy."

Hercules watched Meg as she walked away. "Isn't she something?"

"You bet," Phil said,. "A real pain in the patella!" He mounted Pegasus. "Hey, we got a job to do. Remember? Thebes is waiting."

"Yeah, I know." A reluctant Hercules climbed onto Pegasus.

As the three resumed their journey, Meg turned to watch them streak skyward and disappear into the clouds.

As Meg proceeded through the woods, the trees grew thicker, the path narrower, giving her an eerie feeling. At length she found her way blocked by a chipmunk and a rabbit. With a *poof*, they turned into Pain and Panic. A smoky tendril reached out and grabbed her. Hades.

"What happened?" he asked. "You were supposed to sign up the River Guardian for my uprising." He drew her closer, glowering.

"It wasn't my fault," Meg pleaded. "It was that Wonder Boy, Hercules."

"Hercules?" Hades, dumbfounded, began a slow burn. "HERCULES?" He let out a long, slow growl.

"Aghhh!" croaked Pain and Panic. They made a run for it, but Hades grabbed them by their tails.

"So you took care of him, eh? Here I'm about to rearrange the cosmos, and the one schlemiel who can louse it up is waltzing around in the woods!" Hades exploded into flames.

"A-A-At least we made him mortal," said Pain. "Didn't we?"

"Lucky for the three of you," Hades drew them into a close circle, "we still have time to correct this egregious oversight. And this time, no foul-ups."

His face contorted into an evil grin, which vanished behind a thick whorl of smoke.

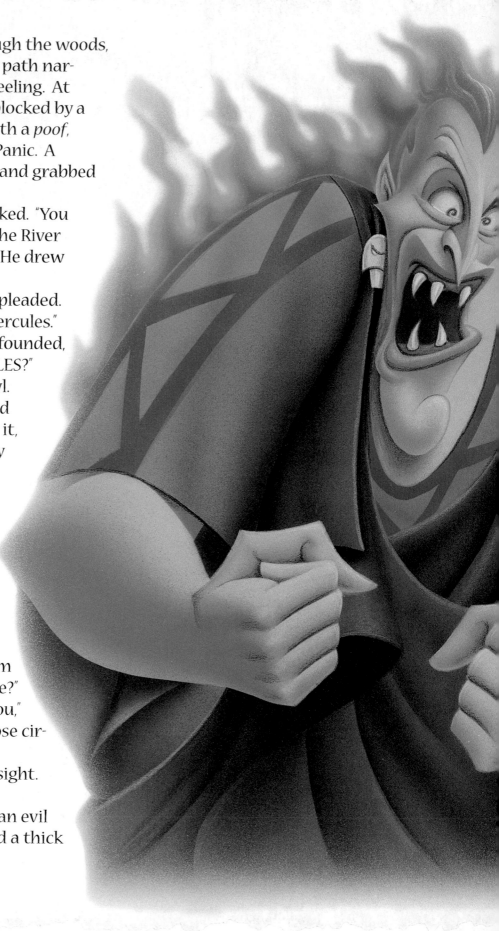

Hercules and Phil, on Pegasus, descended through the clouds to the vast Greek city of Thebes. They made their way through streets teeming with people.

"Stick close to me, kid," said Phil. "The city is a dangerous place."

A crowd of Thebans, all with gloomy faces, stood around a fountain, complaining of recent catastrophes: fires, floods, earthquakes, and the rising crime rate. Hercules saw his chance. "Er, excuse me. It, uh, seems that what you folks need is a hero."

A fat man eyed him skeptically. "And who are you?"

"I'm Hercules, and, uh, I happen to be ... a hero."

"Just what we need. Another chariot chaser."

The crowd chuckled and scoffed, which angered Phil. "Hey, this kid is the genuine article."

"Hold on," said one of the bystanders. "Aren't you the goat-man who trained Achilles?"

"Yeah, that's the guy," said the fat man. "Hey, fella, ya missed a spot on those heels!"

Now furious, Phil butted the man to the ground, and Hercules was forced to break up their fighting.

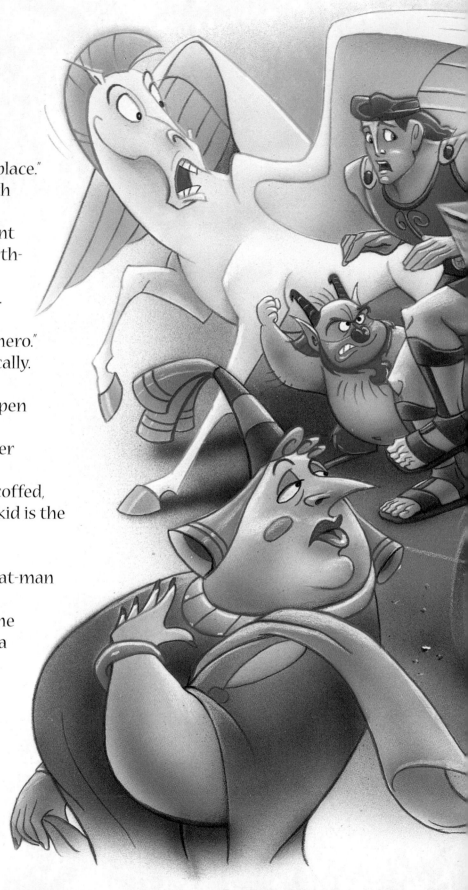

At that very moment a commotion
stirred through the crowd. Hercules
looked over to see Meg calling
frantically, "Help, please! There's been
an accident."

He rushed to her. "What's wrong?"

"Hercules, thank goodness you're
here. There are two little boys
trapped under a rock slide!"

"Kids trapped?" said Hercules.
"Great!"

"I see you're all choked up."

Hercules didn't bother to explain.
"Come on!" He hauled Meg onto Pegasus.

"No, please," she cried, "I'm afraid of . . ."

Pegasus swooshed into the air.

". . . h-heights!" Meg cried. She closed her
eyes and clung tightly to Hercules.

Pegasus landed next to a deep gorge,
and Hercules raced down its steep sides.
He could hear the boys' shouts: "We're
suffocating. Help, call IX-I-I!"

As the crowd watched from the edge
of the canyon, Hercules raised a heavy
boulder that had pinned down the
victims. Meg watched, astounded, as he
lifted it above his head. But the
crowd seemed unimpressed and
gave only a smattering of applause
as the boys scampered out of the
hole.

"Jeepers, mister, you're really
strong!"

"Be more careful next time,"
said Hercules.

The boys, scurrying
up the hill, stopped
short when they ran into
Hades, who was snacking
on worms from a bowl.
"Stirring performance, boys. I
was really moved."

The "boys" turned back into
Pain and Panic and chuckled to
each other. "Jeepers, mister!"

"And how about Meg, our
leading lady?" said Hades.
"I'd give her two thumbs
up!" As he gestured, his
thumbs began to blaze.

Phil hurried down to the canyon floor; Hercules greeted him, beaming. "I did great! They even applauded. Sort of."

There came a high-pitched hissing sound. Phil stood silent, listening. "I hate to burst your bubble, kid, but that ain't applause."

The hissing grew louder. It was coming from the cave that had been covered by the boulders.

With a violent crack of lightning, a gigantic dragonlike creature emerged from the cave. The dreaded Hydra!

From a safe place, Phil coached as Hercules struggled with the Hydra. He tossed a boulder at the beast, but the monster caught the huge rock in its jaws and crunched it to pieces.

With a swift lunge, the Hydra snapped up Hercules in its jaws and swallowed him. The crowd, at the canyon rim, watched as Hercules slashed his way out. Moments later the huge head dropped in front of the crowd, and the beheaded Hydra's body lay lifeless. This time the Thebans applauded with more enthusiasm.

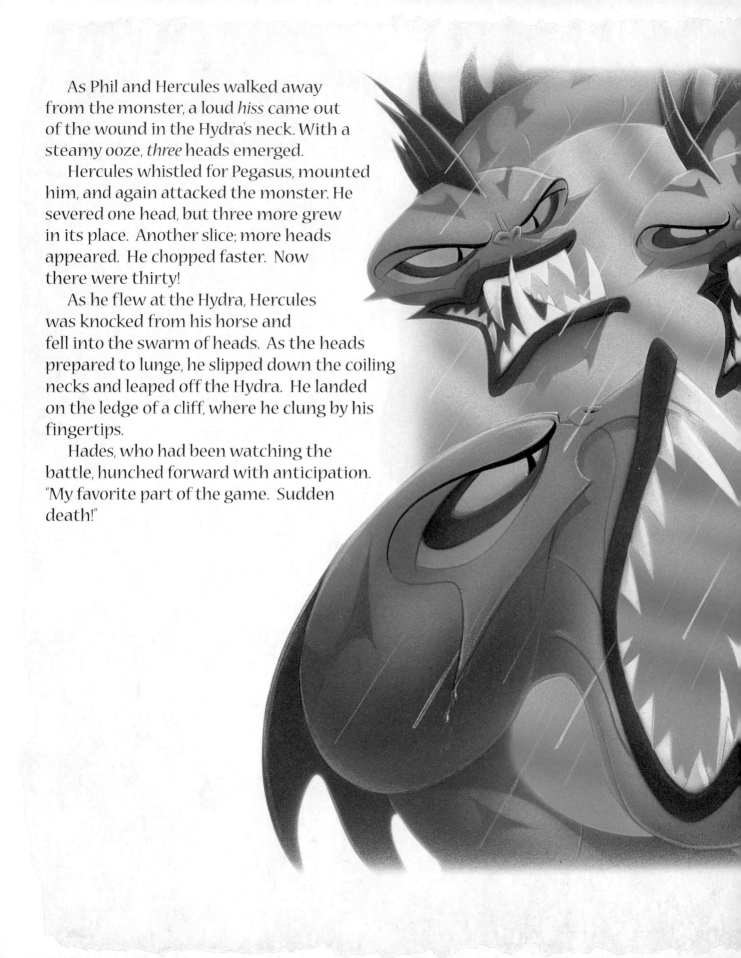

As Phil and Hercules walked away from the monster, a loud *hiss* came out of the wound in the Hydra's neck. With a steamy ooze, *three* heads emerged.

Hercules whistled for Pegasus, mounted him, and again attacked the monster. He severed one head, but three more grew in its place. Another slice; more heads appeared. He chopped faster. Now there were thirty!

As he flew at the Hydra, Hercules was knocked from his horse and fell into the swarm of heads. As the heads prepared to lunge, he slipped down the coiling necks and leaped off the Hydra. He landed on the ledge of a cliff, where he clung by his fingertips.

Hades, who had been watching the battle, hunched forward with anticipation. "My favorite part of the game. Sudden death!"

The monster pinned Hercules to the side of the cliff. All thirty heads moved to attack the trapped hero. He paused for a moment to think, then, summoning all his strength, smashed his fists into the mountainside and the entire hillside collapsed, burying the Hydra and Hercules.

A hush settled over the crowd. "There goes another one," mourned Phil. "Just like Achilles."

Meg closed her eyes in despair. Hades cackled with glee. "Game, set, MATCH!"

Just then came a faint scratching sound from the mountain of rocks. One of the Hydra's talons poked out from the rubble. It opened and a figure crawled out. It was none other than Hercules!

The crowd cheered wildly and hoisted Hercules on their shoulders. He grinned at Phil. "You'll have to admit, *that* was pretty heroic!"

"Ya did it, kid!" shouted Phil. "Ya won by a landslide!"

From that day on Hercules was a superhero. Throughout the city, merchants sold souvenirs depicting the hero's exploits.

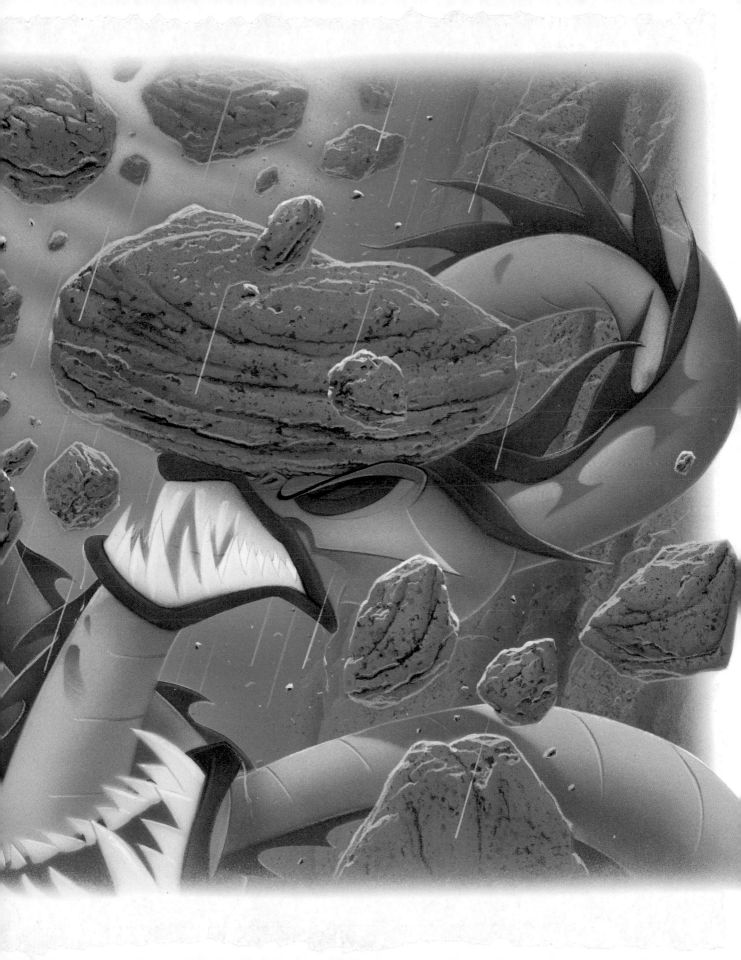

O n a hill above the amphitheater, Hades fumed to Meg, "I can't believe it. I throw everything I've got at him, and it doesn't even ..."

Hades stopped short and stared at Pain's feet, "YOU'RE WEARING *HIS* MERCHANDISE?"

Meg giggled at his wrath. "Hades, Wonder Boy's hitting every curve you throw."

Hades glowered. "Maybe I haven't been throwing the *right* curves, Meg, my sweet."

"I've done my part," said Meg.

He reminded her of how she'd sold her soul to save her former boyfriend.

"It's your freedom, Meg, my sweet. Read my lips ... your *freedom.*"

❖ ❖ ❖

After beating the Hydra, Hercules continued his heroics: subduing monsters and overcoming disasters. After a string of successes, he and Pegasus again paid a visit to the temple of Zeus to report how famous he'd become.

Zeus looked pleased. "I'm proud of you, Son."

"I've waited a long time for this day."

"*What* day?" asked Zeus.

"The day I rejoin the gods."

A shadow crossed Zeus's face. "Sorry, Son. Being famous does not make you a true hero."

"What more can I do?"

"Look inside your heart," said Zeus.

Frustrated by his father's words, Hercules took no pleasure in the fruits of his fame.

In the depths of his depression, Meg appeared, suggesting they play hooky from Phil's heavy celebrity schedule.

After a glorious day together, Hercules and Meg wandered, hand in hand, through his lush terraced gardens.

As they sat by the fountain, two birds, unobserved by Hercules, landed on a nearby pedestal. They morphed into Pain and Panic. "Get the goods!" they whispered to Meg.

Meg winced and rose to continue strolling.

At the reflection pool, Hercules stopped to gaze at a shooting star. "When I was a kid, I used to dream of being like everyone else."

"You wanted to be petty and dishonest?"

"Everybody's not like that." He cupped his hands on her shoulders. "*You're* not like that."

Flustered, Meg drew away.

"Until I met you," said Hercules. "I felt so alone."

"Sometimes it's better to be alone. Then no one can hurt you."

"Meg, I would never hurt you." Hercules moved close and put his arms around her.

Meg put her head against Hercules' chest. "And I don't want to hurt *you*. So let's both do ourselves a favor and stop this before . . ."

They looked up to see a furious Phil circling on Pegasus, shining a lantern on the couple.

Pegasus landed in the garden and snorted at Meg.

"I've been looking all over town!" shouted Phil.

"It's my fault," said Meg.

"You're already on my list, sister. Don't make it worse." Phil turned to Hercules. "And *you're* gonna get the workout of your life!"

"I'll see you tomorrow, Meg," said Hercules. "Meanwhile ..." He plucked a

flower from a tree branch and handed it to Meg, giving her a light kiss on the cheek. And with dreamy glances the lovers parted.

Still in a lovesick trance, Hercules paid no mind to where he was guiding Pegasus. Phil climbed onto Hercules' shoulders. "Watch it. Keep your goo-goo eyes on the—"

Thwack! Phil was caught by a tree branch and knocked for a loop. Hercules and Pegasus sailed off, oblivious of Phil, who had tumbled into a clump of bushes.

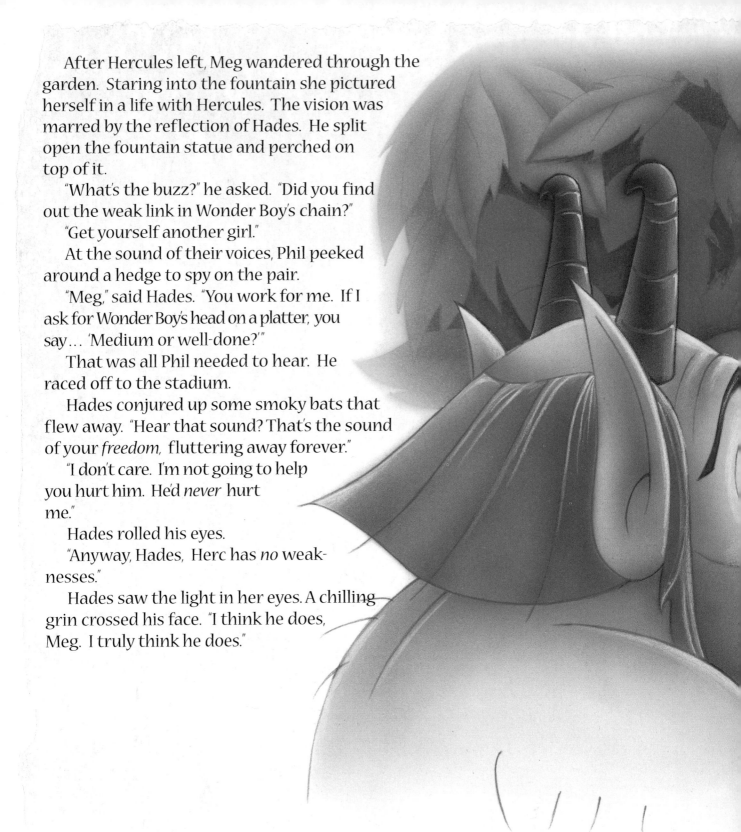

After Hercules left, Meg wandered through the garden. Staring into the fountain she pictured herself in a life with Hercules. The vision was marred by the reflection of Hades. He split open the fountain statue and perched on top of it.

"What's the buzz?" he asked. "Did you find out the weak link in Wonder Boy's chain?"

"Get yourself another girl."

At the sound of their voices, Phil peeked around a hedge to spy on the pair.

"Meg," said Hades. "You work for me. If I ask for Wonder Boy's head on a platter, you say… 'Medium or well-done?'"

That was all Phil needed to hear. He raced off to the stadium.

Hades conjured up some smoky bats that flew away. "Hear that sound? That's the sound of your *freedom,* fluttering away forever."

"I don't care. I'm not going to help you hurt him. He'd *never* hurt me."

Hades rolled his eyes.

"Anyway, Hades, Herc has *no* weaknesses."

Hades saw the light in her eyes. A chilling grin crossed his face. "I think he does, Meg. I truly think he does."

At the Olympic stadium, Phil chased after Hercules. "Kid, we gotta talk."

"That Meg, she is something else!" Hercules did a handstand on the high bars.

"Will you come down and listen?"

"How can I come down when I'm feeling so *up*!" He did a spectacular vault and disappeared into the clouds.

◆ ◆ ◆

Pegasus, watching Hercules' workout, heard a low whistle. A beautiful female winged horse was standing in the doorway of a nearby barn. She winked and motioned.

Eagerly he followed her into the barn. But when Pegasus was inside, the filly split in two. It was Pain and Panic. "Gotcha!"

When Hercules returned to earth, Phil again tried to warn him. "Herc, she's a *fraud*!"

"I know you're upset, but ..."

"She's a two-timing, scheming ..."

"Shut up!" Hercules shoved Phil aside.

Phil stormed off.

"Wait, Phil, I ... I'm sorry. I ..."

"That's it, kid. I'm hopping the first barge home."

"Go ahead. Who needs you?"

Phil looked back at Hercules sadly. "You're no champ. You're a *chump*!"

Hurt and puzzled by Phil's words, Hercules stood in the empty stadium.

Hades appeared before him. "Name is Hades, Lord of the Dead. How ya doin'?" Hercules kept walking.

"I'd be eternally grateful if you'd take a day off from this hero business. Just one day?"

"You're out of your mind."

Hades leered at him. "Well, I *do* have some leverage...."

He snapped his fingers. Meg appeared, bound by wisps of smoke.

"Let her go!" Hercules leaped at Hades but went right through him, as if he were a ghost.

"Here's the deal," said Hades. "Give up your strength for twenty-four hours and Meg will go free."

Hercules looked doubtful. "People are going to get hurt, right?"

Hades moved toward Meg. "Isn't your little smooshy-face here more important?"

Hades squeezed Meg tighter.

Hercules could not bear to see Meg suffer. "You have to swear she'll be safe from any harm."

"Meg is safe; otherwise you get your strength back, yadda-yadda."

They shook hands and at once the color faded from Hercules' body; he felt his strength draining. When Hades threw him a barbell, it floored him easily.

Hades snapped his fingers. Meg's bonds fell away. He turned to Hercules. "Isn't she a fantastic actress?"

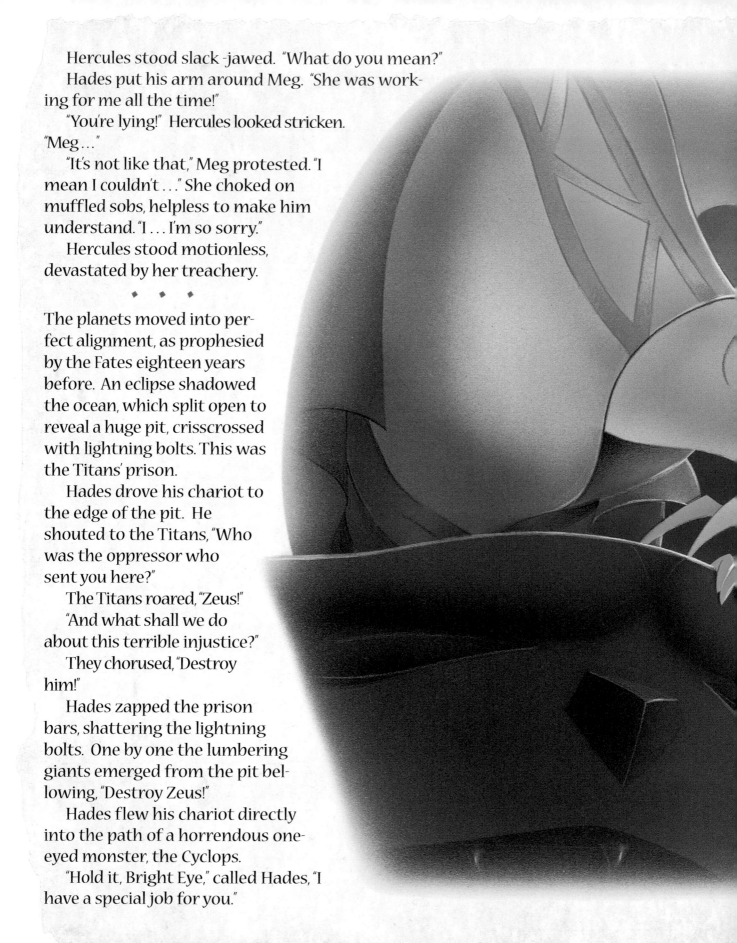

Hercules stood slack-jawed. "What do you mean?"

Hades put his arm around Meg. "She was working for me all the time!"

"You're lying!" Hercules looked stricken. "Meg..."

"It's not like that," Meg protested. "I mean I couldn't..." She choked on muffled sobs, helpless to make him understand. "I... I'm so sorry."

Hercules stood motionless, devastated by her treachery.

◆　◆　◆

The planets moved into perfect alignment, as prophesied by the Fates eighteen years before. An eclipse shadowed the ocean, which split open to reveal a huge pit, crisscrossed with lightning bolts. This was the Titans' prison.

Hades drove his chariot to the edge of the pit. He shouted to the Titans, "Who was the oppressor who sent you here?"

The Titans roared, "Zeus!"

"And what shall we do about this terrible injustice?"

They chorused, "Destroy him!"

Hades zapped the prison bars, shattering the lightning bolts. One by one the lumbering giants emerged from the pit bellowing, "Destroy Zeus!"

Hades flew his chariot directly into the path of a horrendous one-eyed monster, the Cyclops.

"Hold it, Bright Eye," called Hades, "I have a special job for you."

Meanwhile . . . on Mount Olympus, Hermes, awakened by the uprising, rushed to tell Zeus and Hera the news. "The Titans are at our gates!" Then he fled to muster the other gods, who put on their armor, grabbed their weapons, and manned their chariots.

Thebes was in flames. The ground rumbled with earthquakes, and over the city came the roar of the Cyclops, "Hercules, where are you?"

The terrified Thebans, running in every direction, were calling for him, too. "Hercules. Come save us!"

From inside the stadium, Meg and Hercules watched the rampant destruction. Hercules, impassive, started outside.

"Stop!" shouted Meg. "Without your strength, you'll be killed."

"There are worse things," said Hercules. He walked past Meg and headed toward the city.

The Cyclops moved in on him. "So, *you're* mighty Hercules," he laughed, and with a great kick sent him flying. Hercules smashed into a wall and fell into a heap.

Meg looked around desperately for help. From a nearby stable she heard a muffled whinnying. Pegasus!

Inside the barn she found the horse bound in ropes. He resisted her angrily until she cried, "Herc's in trouble!"

She freed Pegasus from his bonds. "We've got to find Phil. He's the only one who can talk sense into him."

Although paralyzed with fear, Meg climbed aboard the steed, who took off like a shot.

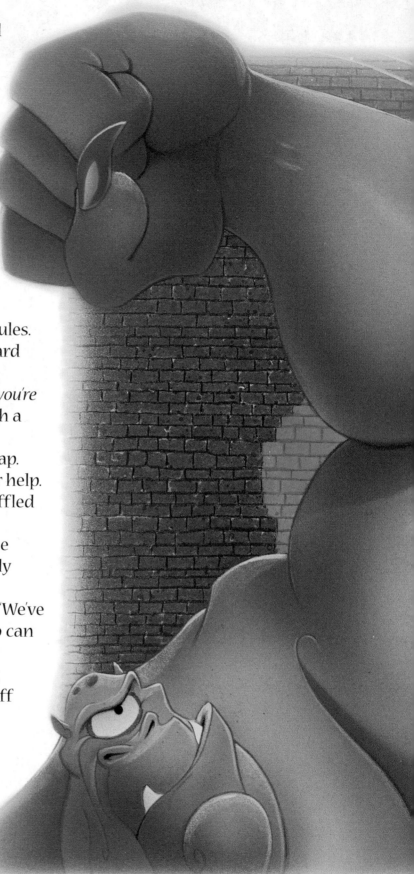

From his throne room, Zeus called for more ammunition, but Hephaestus, forger of thunderbolts, had been captured. Zeus hurled his last thunderbolt at the approaching Titans. It glanced off the shield of the Rock Titan, and the enemy surrounded him, shouting, "Destroy Zeus!"

The Lava Titan belched up a molten stream, which cascaded around Zeus. The Ice Titan blew the lava cold. It hardened, encasing Zeus's body.

As the god struggled to free himself, Hades flew in on his chariot, singing out, "Oh, Zeus-y, I'm home!"

"Hades," groaned Zeus. "I should have known you were behind this."

Hades watched the lava rise around the now powerless god. "Right you are, bolt boy." He zapped a fireball from his finger. "From now on, *I* call the shots."

◆　◆　◆

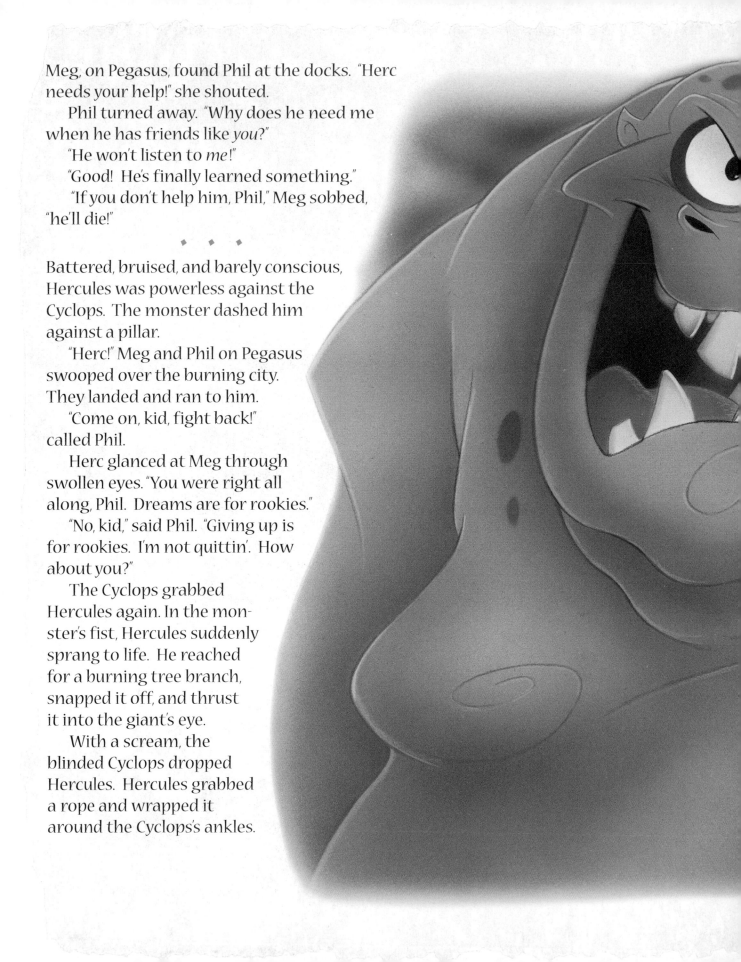

Meg, on Pegasus, found Phil at the docks. "Herc needs your help!" she shouted.

Phil turned away. "Why does he need me when he has friends like *you*?"

"He won't listen to *me*!"

"Good! He's finally learned something."

"If you don't help him, Phil," Meg sobbed, "he'll die!"

◆ ◆ ◆

Battered, bruised, and barely conscious, Hercules was powerless against the Cyclops. The monster dashed him against a pillar.

"Herc!" Meg and Phil on Pegasus swooped over the burning city. They landed and ran to him.

"Come on, kid, fight back!" called Phil.

Herc glanced at Meg through swollen eyes. "You were right all along, Phil. Dreams are for rookies."

"No, kid," said Phil. "Giving up is for rookies. I'm not quittin'. How about you?"

The Cyclops grabbed Hercules again. In the monster's fist, Hercules suddenly sprang to life. He reached for a burning tree branch, snapped it off, and thrust it into the giant's eye.

With a scream, the blinded Cyclops dropped Hercules. Hercules grabbed a rope and wrapped it around the Cyclops's ankles.

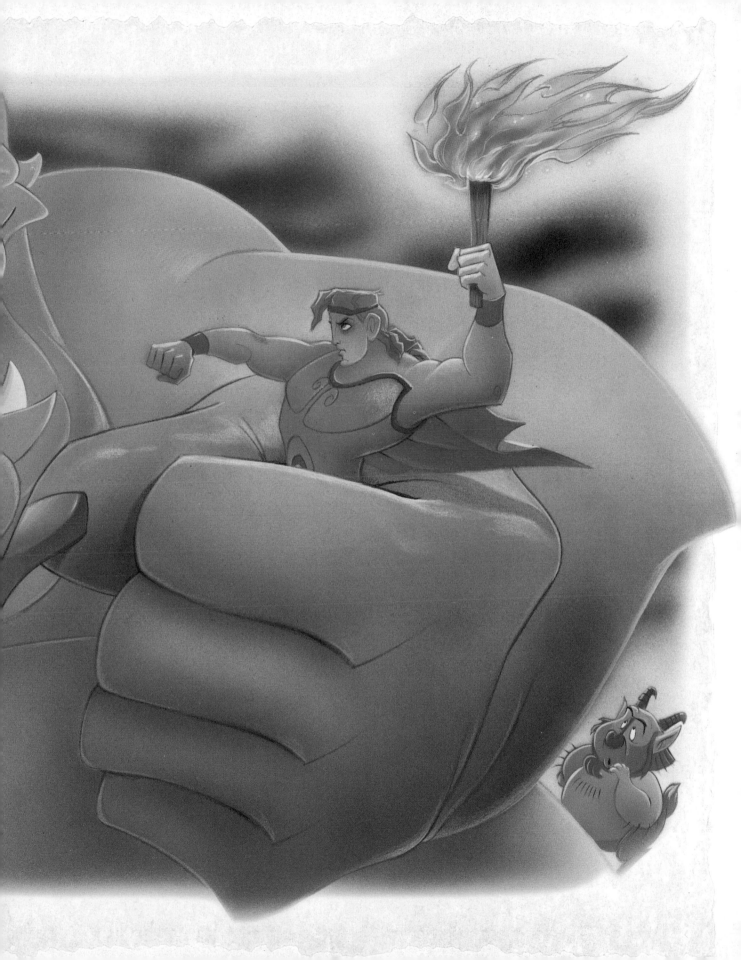

Groping for his prey, the Cyclops tripped on the rope and fell against two huge columns. Then he tumbled into the sea.

One of the weakened columns teetered and began falling toward Hercules.

"Look out!" Meg dashed to push Hercules out of the way; the column fell on her instead.

Hercules pulled with all his might, but the column would not budge. He tried again, straining. Little by little his color came back.

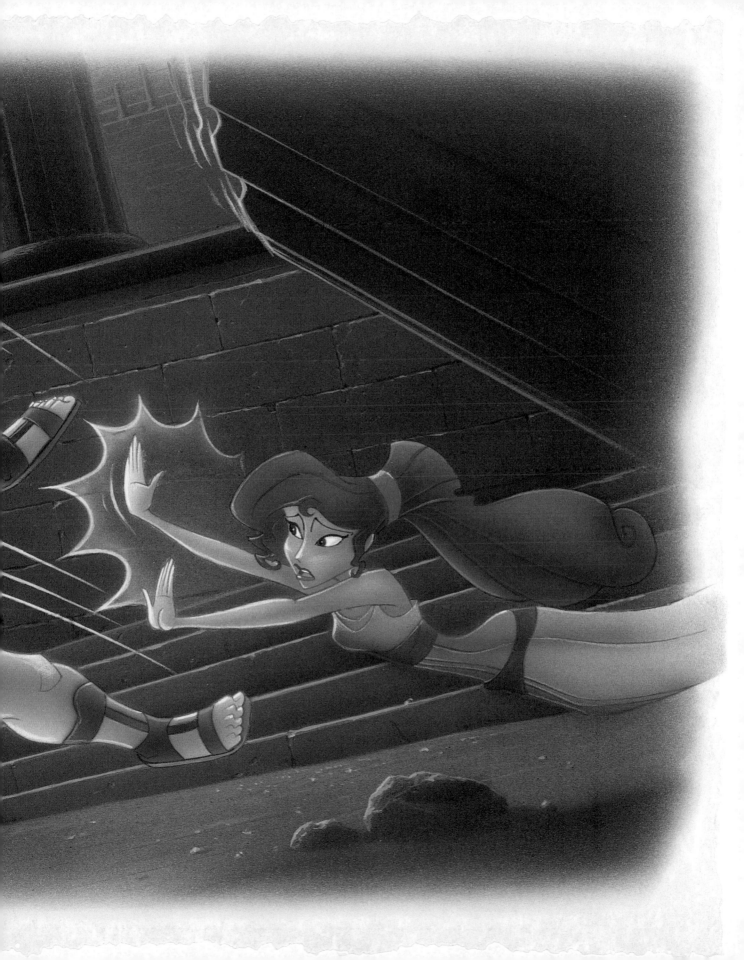

"What . . . what's happening?" With one arm he hoisted the pillar into the air. His godlike strength had returned!

"Hades . . . his deal is broken," gasped Meg, who was badly injured. "He promised I wouldn't get hurt."

Hercules cradled Meg in his arms. "You . . . you saved me. But why?"

"I guess people do crazy things when they're in love."

"L-Love? Oh, Meg . . . Meg . . . I . . . I . . ."

From a distance they saw lightning and heard thunder from Olympus.

"You . . . you can still stop Hades," said Meg weakly, "but there's not much time."

"I'll watch over her, kid," said Phil. Hercules gently laid Meg in his friend's arms.

Hercules and Pegasus sped toward Mount Olympus. They dashed in and out among the gods, breaking their chains and freeing them. Hercules called to Hades, "This ought to even up the odds."

"Yea, Hercules!" With a defiant yell the gods grabbed their swords and armor and launched into battle against the Titans.

As Hercules sped toward Zeus, the Lava Titan spewed a boiling stream, and the Ice Titan spit chilling shards, but Hercules raced right through them. He leaped off Pegasus and attacked the frozen lava that surrounded Zeus.

"Thank you, my boy," said Zeus. He signaled to Hephaestus, who tossed him a load of thunderbolts. "Now watch your old man work." He hurled the lightning charges at the Titans, who shrieked and scattered.

A supercharged Hercules, on Pegasus, swept in front of the retreating Titans. Dismounting, he grabbed the Tornado Titan by its tail and twirled it like a lasso. Then, using it like a vacuum cleaner, he sucked up the rest of the Titans and hurled them all into space.

He turned to see Hades, in his chariot. The Lord of the Dead called, "Gotta go collect my consolation prize." He dived into the clouds. "A friend of yours. I know she's *dying* to see me."

Hercules frowned; then it hit him. "MEG!"

Hercules flew on Pegasus toward Thebes, praying it wouldn't be too late.

Landing, he rushed to find Meg. Phil's tearful face told the story.
"Meg! No!" Hercules lifted Meg's limp body into his arms.
"Sorry, kid," said Phil. "Some things ya just can't change."
"Oh, yes, I can." Hercules headed for Pegasus. "Yes, I can!"

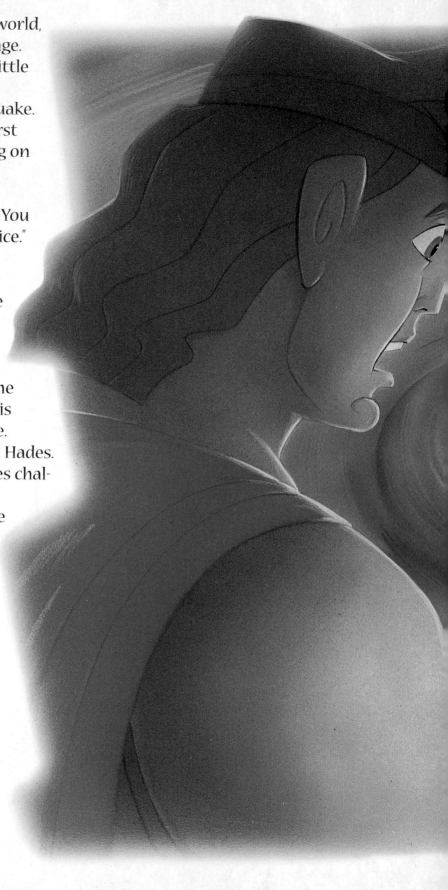

Inside his palace in the Underworld, Hades exploded into rockets of rage. "We were so close. And then our little *nut*-Meg had to . . ."

Suddenly the walls began to quake. The gates of the throne room burst open, and in came Hercules, riding on the watchdog Cerberus.

"Where's Meg?" he demanded.

"Wonder Boy, you're too much. You know no one visits here . . . by choice."

"Let her go!"

Through the arch of a large stone doorway Hercules could see a swirling mass of souls moving toward a skull-like opening. He caught sight of Meg.

"Meg!" Hercules reached into the swirl but pulled back in horror. His hands and arms had begun to age.

"No, no, mustn't touch," mocked Hades.

"You like making deals," Hercules challenged. "Take me in Meg's place."

"Hmm," Hades considered. "The son of my hated rival trapped forever in the river of death?"

"Going once . . . ," said Hercules.

"Is there a downside to this?"

"Going twice . . ."

"Okay, okay. You fish Meg out, she goes, you stay."

◆　　◆　　◆

Hercules dived into the vortex of souls.
Caught in the swirl, he began to age. Even
so, he swam after Meg. By the time he
reached her he was almost a skeleton. He
reached out his bony hand and grabbed
the woman he had promised to protect.

Carrying Meg, Hercules gained a
handhold on the ledge that overlooked
the pit of death. As he clung there, his
skeletal form slowly turned back to
normal. Then his body began to radi-
ate with the godly glow he had lost as
an infant!

Hades looked on, horrified. "You
can't be alive. You'd have to be a …
a …"

"A god?" said Pain and Panic.

Hercules carried Meg out of the pit
and past Hades, who tried to block him.
"You can't *do* this to me!"

In response, Hercules backhanded
Hades and strode on. Hades pleaded,
"Can't we talk? You know, god to god?"
Hercules merely glared at him.

Hades fell to his knees, begging.
"Maybe your dad will blow this one off?"
Teetering on the edge of the pit, he
implored Meg's spirit, "Meg, talk to him!"

Hercules lunged at Hades, knocking him
into the pit.

"Nooooo!" the god shrieked as he swirled
into the mass of spirits. "Get your slimy souls
off me!" But the unrelenting spirits dragged
Hades down into their midst.

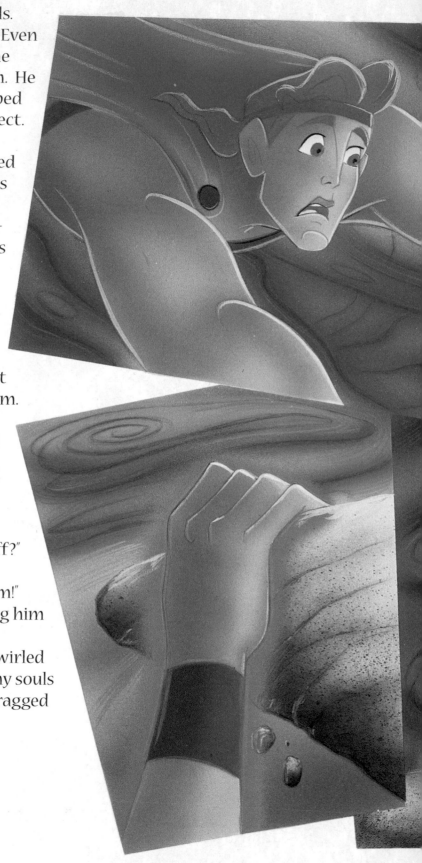

With Phil and Pegasus standing by, Hercules guided Meg's spirit to her lifeless body. As the two melded, Meg's eyelids fluttered, then opened. Hercules helped Meg to her feet, then they embraced.

As they held each other, bolts of lightning struck the ground beneath them, and a cloud billowed under their feet.

The cloud began to rise toward the heavens. It settled at the bottom of a lofty stairway that led to the gates of Mount Olympus.

As Hercules started up the stairs, the entire pantheon of gods gave him a standing ovation.

Hera greeted him. "We're so proud of you, Son."

"Mother?"

The goddess nodded and hugged him.

"Fine work, my boy," said Zeus. "You're a true hero."

"You risked everything," said Hera, "to rescue this young woman."

Zeus crossed his arms over his broad chest. "A true hero isn't measured by the size of his strength but by the strength of his heart."

Hercules grinned toward Phil and Meg.

"And now, at last, my son," said Zeus, "you can come home."

The gates of Olympus opened. Meg looked up at Hercules, her eyes glistening. "Congratulations, Wonder Boy. You'll make one terrific god."

Hercules' smile faded. He turned to Zeus. "Father, this is the moment I've always dreamed of. But…"

He paused and looked at Meg. "Life without Meg, even an immortal one, would be … an eternal waste of time."

Hercules took Meg's hand. She brightened through her tears.

"I … I wish to stay on Earth with her." He smiled. "I finally know where I belong."

Zeus's face clouded. He looked to Hera questioningly. Hera took his hand and nodded her approval.

The gods cheered as Pegasus carried Herc, Meg, and Phil back to Earth.

Meg looked up to the heavens. Zeus had formed a cluster of stars into a constellation, depicting a heroic Hercules. Reaching from the firmament, the hand of Zeus snatched a shooting star and placed it at the heart of the constellation.

Hercules felt his chest swell. At last he knew what his father meant: heroic deeds are born in the heart.

◆　◆　◆

And so we muses end our story of Hercules, the greatest hero of all time.

BEHIND THE SCENES
WITH HERCULES PRODUCER ALICE DEWEY

In the fall of 1994, I joined a small group of Disney artists to develop the film *Hercules*. I had always loved the beauty of Greek art and was enthralled by the stories of the gods and heroes in the Greek myths. Besides, I would be reunited with directors John Musker and Ron Clements, with whom I had worked on *Aladdin*. I knew they were not only extremely talented filmmakers, but also very funny people.

Ron and John chose *Hercules* for their next movie script because they were enticed by two major ideas. Ron explains that Hercules "was a common-man's hero, perhaps the first superhero. He's kind of a comic book character, and we wanted to get that sense of fun and action into the movie." The other appealing factor was that the characters in Greek myths have a fantasy aspect that makes them ideal for animated films. Satyrs, centaurs, griffins, monsters, and flying horses are the types of characters that a Disney cartoon can bring alive better than a live-action film.

Played by Tate Donovan and Susan Egan, respectively, Hercules is an affable and earnest hero, while Meg is smart as well as vulnerable.

Early in the process, an English artist, Gerald Scarfe, joined the team. John admired his ability to draw caricatures, and we were looking to explore a fanciful and powerful design for the gods and magical creatures in the movie. We visited Gerald several times in London, and he visited our Los Angeles and Paris studios. It was a great thrill to watch him draw. His caricatures are very large and he likes to draw standing up, using paper as big as a poster. This allows him to use his entire arm to sweep over the paper. The result is a forceful, confident expression with a dynamic graphic line. Gerald continued on the movie for several years—at first exploring ideas on his own, and later working back and forth with the animators on ideas for their characters' designs. Gerald tells us there's a moment "when a character arrives. Various characters come in and audition on your drawing board, but they don't look right. Suddenly one arrives and you think, That's him. That's the guy."

In animation, all the designs must be worked out early, so when the hundreds of artists start on the actual scenes that you see in the theater, the characters are defined and ready for them. What will our hero look like? What does a centaur look like? How would you draw Mount Olympus? Andreas Deja, the supervising animator of the adult Hercules, says, "The interesting thing about our movie is that it's so stylized. Hercules doesn't look like your

Played by the improvisational James Woods, Hades charms and connives in a brilliant show of comic villainy.

typical Disney prince, a sort of good-looking guy. He looks like a Greek vase illustration and a handsome modern guy at the same time. He's got that straight nose, and those curly lips, and he just looks like a Greek god." That's one of the wonderful things about animated movies. Every character and background you see and all the sounds you hear are decisions we make to create a believable world for you, the audience.

One of the highlights of working on this movie was a research trip we took to Greece and Turkey. For two weeks, a Greek scholar took the directors, key artists, and me on a remarkable tour. We soaked up the landscape, the colors, and the architecture of Greece. So much of what we had read about now became a visual feast laid out before us. When Art Director Andy Gaskill, Layout Supervisor Rasoul Azadani, and Background Supervisor Tom Cardone returned to the film studio, they had hundreds of photos, sketches, and hours of videotape to inspire their work on the movie's settings.

Hercules' trainer, Phil, is a satyr—half goat, half man—played with crustiness and affection by Danny DeVito.

Often in mythology, the hero fights a tremendous monster. Our story of Hercules is no different: a fierce Hydra threatens the city of Thebes and Hercules bravely faces this monster with just his sword, his wits, and the help of Pegasus, his flying horse. Hercules tries to defeat the Hydra by cutting off her head. But the Hydra is a beast who grows three heads every time one of the heads is cut off. To help us animate such a difficult drawing task, we turned to the computer. Artists, led by Roger Gould in our Computer Generated Imagery department, created an exciting action scene in which Hercules scrambles to defeat this monster. "It's enormous," Roger says, describing the battle. "At one point in the battle he chops off one head and thinks, Hey, I'm doing great! Of course, it only gets worse, with more and more heads popping out. Hercules is forced on the defensive; he keeps slicing even though he knows it's a bad idea. He ends up flying around on Pegasus inside a living jungle of Hydra necks, as the snarling heads gang up to attack him."

Animated movies require the talents of hundreds and hundreds of artists. It is a privilege to be able to watch the movie grow from the script to the story-boards to the layouts and animation, then adding the special effects and color to create eventually the final film that you see in the theater. For several years, artists in Los Angeles and Paris worked patiently at their desks—some with computers, some with pencils, some with paintbrushes—to make frame by frame drawings that bring the world of ancient Greece to life for us today.

Zeus is the blustery, folksy, yet formidable Lord of the Universe, richly voiced by Rip Torn.

Printed in the United States of America.

ISBN 0-7868-3126-X (trade)—ISBN 0-7868-5050-7 (lib. bdg.)
Library of Congress Catalog Card Number: 96-71817

Adapted from
Walt Disney Pictures' **HERCULES**
MUSIC BY Alan Menken LYRICS BY David Zippel
ORIGINAL SCORE BY Alan Menken
SCREENPLAY BY Ron Clements & John Musker,
Bob Shaw & Don McEnery AND Irene Mecchi
PRODUCED BY Alice Dewey
AND John Musker & Ron Clements
DIRECTED BY John Musker & Ron Clements
DISTRIBUTED BY BUENA VISTA PICTURES DISTRIBUTION © DISNEY ENTERPRISES, INC.

The artwork for each picture
is prepared using acrylic and guache.

This book is set in
14-point Nueva Roman.